BIG BIRD'S DAY ON THE FARM

By Cathi Rosenberg-Turow

Illustrated by Maggie Swanson

Featuring Jim Henson's Sesame Street Muppets

Inspired by SESAME STREET PRESENTS: FOLLOW THAT BIRD,
screenplay by Tony Geiss and Judy Freudberg

This educational book was created in cooperation with the Children's Television Workshop, producers of Sesame Street. Children do not have to watch the television show to benefit from this book. Workshop revenues from this product will be used to help support CTW educational projects.

A SESAME STREET/GOLDEN PRESS BOOK

Published by Western Publishing Company, Inc. in conjunction with Children's Television Workshop.

© 1985 Children's Television Workshop. Sesame Street Muppets © Muppets, Inc. 1985. All rights reserved. Printed in the U.S.A. by Western Publishing Company, Inc. No part of this book may be reproduced or copied in any form without written permission from the publisher. Sesame Street® and the Sesame Street sign are trademarks and service marks of Children's Television Workshop. GOLDEN®, GOLDEN & DESIGN®, GOLDEN PRESS®, and A LITTLE GOLDEN BOOK® are trademarks of Western Publishing Company, Inc. Library of Congress Catalog Card Number: 84-72876 ISBN 0-307-02022-3/ISBN 0-307-60283-4 (lib. bdg.)   G H I J

BIG BIRD was on his way to Sesame Street when he saw a sign at a fork in the road. It said, "No Through Road."

"What a funny name for a road," said Big Bird.

"Maybe this is the way to Sesame Street," said Big Bird as he walked along the dirt road.

"Hi there!" Big Bird greeted a flock of chickens pecking on the road. "Do you mind if I join you for dinner?"

Big Bird looked up and saw a little girl staring at him. "You're the biggest chicken I've ever seen," she said.

"I'm not a big chicken. I'm a Big Bird," he said.

"Nice to meet you, Big Bird. I'm Ruthie, and this is my brother Floyd."

"Would you like to visit our farm, Big Bird?" asked Ruthie.

"Oh, thanks," he answered with a yawn. "It's too late for me to get all the way to Sesame Street today."

Ruthie and Floyd took Big Bird to the barn. They made him a soft nest out of hay.

As they tucked Big Bird in, Floyd asked, "Will you stay and play with us tomorrow? You could help us feed the animals."

"I'd like that," Big Bird answered.

"When the rooster crows, you'll know it's time to get up," said Ruthie.

Then they kissed him good night.

Big Bird waited and waited for the rooster to crow.
"Maybe he's taking a nap," Big Bird thought as he fell
asleep.
"Cockadoodledooooo!"
Big Bird woke up and saw the sun coming up over the
henhouse.

After breakfast Ruthie and Floyd took Big Bird to see the cows.

"The first chore we do every morning is milk the cows and feed them hay," said Ruthie.

"Gee!" said Big Bird. "On Sesame Street we get our milk from Hooper's Store."

Next they went to the henhouse. Ruthie and Floyd showed Big Bird how to take eggs out of the nests gently and carry them carefully in an egg basket.

"Gee," said Big Bird. "On Sesame Street we get our eggs in cardboard cartons."

Then Ruthie and Floyd took Big Bird to the pigpen.
"Here's your breakfast," said Ruthie to the pigs.
    "You look like someone I know back home," Big Bird
said to one little piggy.

When they went out to the field to feed the horses, Big Bird carried the bag of oats. They poured the oats into troughs for the horses.

"Bert likes oatmeal, too," said Big Bird. "He would love it here!"

"Now we'll show you where honey comes from," said Ruthie, leading Big Bird out in the field to the beehives. "The bees gather nectar from the flowers, and they bring it here to their hive. Then they turn the nectar into honey."

"Don't pet the bees," said Floyd.

Then Big Bird, Ruthie, and Floyd went to the apple orchard.

"I know how to pick these apples fast," said Big Bird.

Without even standing on tiptoe, Big Bird could reach every apple on the tree.

In the garden Ruthie and Floyd picked cucumbers and tomatoes off the vines. Big Bird couldn't believe it when Ruthie pulled a carrot right out of the ground.

"Gee," he said. "On Sesame Street we get our vegetables from Mr. MacIntosh's fruit-and-vegetable stand."

Now the sun was high in the sky. They went to the house for a delicious farm lunch.

Then it was time for Big Bird to go home.

"Come and visit us again," said Ruthie and Floyd, waving good-by.

"Thanks for everything," said Big Bird. "I had a wonderful day on the farm." He looked up the road, then down. "By the way," he said, "can you tell me how to get to Sesame Street?"